SONGS

FOR SOLO VOICE
AND PIANO

Wolfgang Amadeus Mozart

DOVER PUBLICATIONS, INC.
New York

Copyright © 1993 by Dover Publications, Inc.

Published in Canada by General Publishing Company, Ltd., 30 Lesmill Road, Don
Mills, Toronto, Ontario.

Published in the United Kingdom by Constable and Company, Ltd., 3 The Lanchesters,
162–164 Fulham Palace Road, London W6 9ER.

This Dover edition, first published in 1993, is a republication of the volume "Serie 7.
Erste Abtheilung. Lieder und Gesänge mit Begleitung des Pianoforte" from *Wolfgang
Amadeus Mozart's Werke. Kritisch durchgesehene Gesammtausgabe,* published by
Breitkopf und Härtel, n.d., in Leipzig. The music in this volume has been reproduced in
its entirety, although the order of the contents has been altered, as explained in the
Publisher's Note. The table of contents has been revised accordingly. English translations
of the German tempo indicators have been added to the main text. The Publisher's Note
has been added and the literal line-for-line translation of the German, Italian and French
texts has been specially prepared for this edition by Stanley Appelbaum.

Manufactured in the United States of America
Dover Publications, Inc., 31 East 2nd Street, Mineola, N.Y. 11501

Library of Congress Cataloging-in-Publication Data

Mozart, Wolfgang Amadeus, 1756–1791.
    [Vocal music. Selections]
    Songs for solo voice and piano / Wolfgang Amadeus Mozart.
    1 score.
    Includes works with chorus, trios, and 6 works misattributed to W. A. Mozart.
    Principally German words.
    Reprint. Originally published: Lieder und Gesänge mit Begleitung des Pianoforte.
Leipzig : Breitkopf & Härtel, before 1881. (Wolfgang Amadeus Mozart's Werke. Serie
7 ; 1. Abt.).
    English translations of the words printed as text.
    ISBN 0-486-27568-X
    1. Vocal music—Scores.   2. Songs with piano.
M3.1.M9D7   1993   92-44249
                                                          CIP
                                                          M

CONTENTS

The years and places are those of composition.

Publisher's Note

THIS DOVER EDITION contains all the music contained in the Breitkopf und Härtel edition of *Mozart's Werke*, Serie 7, "Lieder und Gesänge mit Begleitung des Pianoforte," published in Leipzig prior to 1881. The order of the contents has been changed to reflect the findings published in the sixth edition, 1964, of the Köchel *Chronologisch-Thematisches Verzeichnis sämtlicher Tonwerke Wolfgang Amade Mozarts*, so that all the authentic Lieder for solo voice and piano (in two cases, mandolin) accompaniment now appear in the chronological order in which they were composed. This body of songs is followed by the two Masonic songs with chorus; two trios, one accompanied, the other a cappella; the aria "Un moto di gioja" (an alternative aria composed for the soprano Adriana Gabrieli ("la Ferrarese") in the role of Susanna in *Le nozze di Figaro* but retained here with its piano accompaniment) and the cantata "Die ihr des unermesslichen Weltalls." These are followed in turn by two songs, K.52 and K.149, arranged or composed either fully or in large measure by Leopold Mozart. The final four works in this volume are spurious and have been misattributed to Mozart. The canzonetta K.152 is a reworking of an aria, "Il caro mio bene" by Josef Mysliveček, whom Mozart had met in Bologna in 1770. K.350, "Wiegenlied," was composed by one Bernhard Flies. K.150 and K.151 exist without benefit of attributed authorship. Köchel's original numbering is retained throughout this edition; however, the revised numbering, according to the sixth edition of the Köchel catalog, is shown in the table of contents as (K⁶) where it differs from the original numbering.

The present corpus of songs demonstrates the same wide emotional range found throughout Mozart's work and covers his entire creative life, from the early K.52 (in the creation of which his father played a large part) to the cantata K.619, a concise yet powerful statement of ethical beliefs. In between the two are to be found pithy examples of Mozart's mastery of this intimate genre. Within the confines of strophic settings whole dramas take place, spiritual tenets are affirmed and trenchant portraits, such as the nasal old lady of "Die Alte," are drawn. Mozart's assured handling of the texts, his understanding of their nuances, the often orchestral effects of the piano writing (for example, the accompaniment to the Ariette "Dans un bois") and the clear influence of operatic techniques (particularly in "Als Luise die Briefe ihres ungetreuen Liebhabers verbrannte") point the way to the great blossoming of the German Lied in the early nineteenth century, even if the present examples are surely modest in scope.

The two songs for solo voice with chorus, K.483 and K.484, are examples of Mozart's compositions associated with his Masonic activities. In style they reflect the simplicity of the new German liturgical music, devised to make musical participation in worship accessible to all, with simple melodies kept within a relatively narrow tessitura. The subject of these songs is clearly Masonic, however. Both Wolfgang and his father Leopold were members of lodges in Vienna and these two compositions were served as ceremonial music for, respectively, the inauguration of a Masonic lodge ("Zur Eröffnung der Meisterloge") and the conclusion of a Master ceremony ("Zum Schluss der Meisterarbeit"). The Masonic demands for secrecy with respect to ceremonies and practices account for the cryptic blanks in the titles of these songs. Both pieces were written for the installation of the Viennese lodge "Zur gekrönten Hoffnung" (Crowned Hope) which opened on 14 January 1786. The "Lied zur Gesellenreise," K.468, was performed on 16 April 1785 at the lodge "Zur wahren Eintracht" (True Concord) at a ceremony during which Leopold Mozart was elevated to the Second Degree, one of three Masonic levels of mastery. The key of this song is B♭, having a key signature of two flats, symbolizing the Second Degree. In Mozart's symbology, E♭, having three flats in its signature (signifying the third and highest Degree), is the key of Knowledge and is the fundamental tonality of *Die Zauberflöte*, Mozart's unambiguously Masonic opera.

Mozart's earthy sense of humor is evident in the comic trio "Das Bändchen," K.441, which celebrates, in a charming rondo, a household event in the life of the Mozarts of true insignificance. The other trio in this volume is a setting of a verse by Pietro Metastasio, "Grazie agl'inganni tuoi" from his libretto *La libertà di Nice*. The composition may not be entirely Mozart's work, but rather an adaptation of a duet of the same name by the Irish tenor and composer Michael Kelly, who was well known to Mozart and who created the roles of Don Curzio and Don Basilio in *Le nozze di Figaro*. Though not falling into the category of songs for solo voice, these two trios have been retained as they originally appeared in the Breitkopf und Härtel edition of the Complete Works. Their presence is illustrative of Mozart's treatment of solo voices in a chamber-music setting.

These thirty-odd songs span Mozart's entire compositional career, although the genre seems to have engaged him only fitfully. The mature songs, from K.472 onwards, were composed in small groups over a short period of time, which is not to suggest textural or thematic relationships, but rather to propose the spontaneity with which these songs were conceived. Indeed, K.472, K.473 and K.474 were all composed on the same day, 7 May 1785, and on 14 January 1791 Mozart wrote the last three songs, K.596, K.597 and K.598. The other songs were composed two or three at a time, usually within a few weeks of each other. A number of years separates each group. Throughout the songs Mozart exhibits work of distinction which lifts the form from the realm of folksong and lays the groundwork for the development of the Lied into a high art form. In preparing this edition it is hoped that singer and audience alike will be charmed and gratified by these delightful miniatures.

SONGS

FOR SOLO VOICE
AND PIANO

An die Freude

K.53

Mässig.
Moderately.

Freu - - de, Kö_ni_gin der Wei_sen, die, mit Blu _ men

um ihr Haupt, dich auf güld_ner Lei_er preisen, ru_hig,

wenn die Bos_heit schnaubt, ru_hig, wenn die Bos_heit schnaubt:

Hö_re mich von dei_nem Thro_ne, Kind der Weis_heit,

de_ren Hand im_mer selbst in___ dei_ne Kro_ne ih_re

schön _ sten   Ro _ sen   band,   ih _ re   schön _ _ sten   Ro _ sen   band.

2.

Rosen, die mit frischen Blättern,
Trotz dem Nord, unsterblich blüh'n,
Trotz dem Südwind, unter Wettern,
Wenn die Wolken Flammen sprüh'n,
Die dein lockicht Haar durchschlingen,
Nicht nur an Cytherens Brust,
Wenn die Grazien dir singen,
Oder bei Lyäens Lust.

3.

Sie bekränzen dich in Zeiten,
Die kein Sonnenblick erhellt,
Sahen dich das Glück bestreiten.
Den Tyrannen unsrer Welt,
Der um seine Riesenglieder
Donnerndes Gewölke zog,
Und mit schrecklichem Gefieder
Zwischen Erd' und Himmel flog.

4.

Dich und deine Rosen sahen
Auch die Gegenden der Nacht
Sich des Todes Throne nahen,
Wo das kalte Schrecken wacht.
Deinen Pfad, wo du gegangen,
Zeichnete das sanfte Licht
Cynthiens mit vollen Wangen,
Die durch schwarze Schatten bricht.

5.

Dir war dieser Herr des Lebens,
War der Tod nicht fürchterlich,
Und er schwenkete vergebens
Seinen Wurfspiess wider dich:
Weil im traurigen Gefilde
Hoffnung dir zur Seite ging
Und mit diamantnem Schilde
Ueber deinem Haupte hing.

6.

Hab' ich meine kühnen Saiten
Dein lautschallend Lob gelehrt,
Das vielleicht in späten Zeiten
Ungeborne Nachwelt hört;
Hab' ich den beblümten Pfaden,
Wo du wandelst, nachgespürt,
Und von stürmischen Gestaden
Einige zu dir geführt:

7.

Göttin, o so sei, ich flehe,
Deinem Dichter immer hold,
Dass er schimmernd Glück verschmähe,
Reich in sich auch ohne Gold;
Dass sein Leben zwar verborgen,
Aber ohne Sklaverei,
Ohne Flecken, ohne Sorgen,
Weisen Freunden theuer sei!

"Wie unglücklich bin ich nit"

K.147

"O heiliges Band"

K. 148

Ariette

"Oiseaux, si tous les ans"

K.307

Ariette
"Dans un bois"
K.308

Singstimme.

Pianoforte.

Dans un bois so_li_tai_re et som bre je_____ me prome
Ein_ sam ging ich_jüngst im Hai_ ne, da_____ ge

nais_____ l'autr' jour, un en_ fant y dormait à l'om bre,
wahrt' ich im Ge_büsch ei_ nen Kna_ben ein_ge_schlum_mert.

c'é _ tait le redou_ta _ _ ble A _ mour,___ c'é _ tait le redou_ta _ ble A
Ach! der bö_se_ A _ _ mor_ war's,___ ach! der bö_se_ A _ mor

mour. J'ap_pro _ _ che, sa beau _ té me flat_ te, mais je de
war's. Wie lag_____ er da so_ schön, so freundlich! doch konnte

8

9

10

11

"Verdankt sei es dem Glanz"

K. 392

Gleichgültig und zufrieden
Indifferent and contented.

1. Ver_dankt sei es dem Glanz der Gro_ssen, dass er mein Nichts mir deut_lich
2. Sie sind mir werth, die en _ gen Grenzen, wo ich so un _ be_trächt_lich
3. Soll mir des Grö _ ssern Un _ muth zei_gen, ich sei nur ei _ ne Klei_nig_
4. Doch lie _ sse sich zu mei _ nem Krei_se ein Gro_sser oh _ ne Falsch her_

zeigt. Mich hat er nie zurück_ge _ sto_ssen, denn mich hat er nie_mals er_reicht. Ich sah viel Kleine nä _ her
bin. Hier seh' ich Stern und Or_den glän_zen, und Band und Stern reisst mich nicht hin. Und auch das gnä_dig_ste Ge_
keit: O Unschuld! dann lehr'du mich schweigen und gieb mir Un _ er_schrockenheit, und prä_ge mir sanfttrö_stend
ab: Er_fahrung! dann mach'du mich wei_se und zeich_ne mei _ ne Grenzen ab, und leh_re mich, niemals zu

geh'n und blieb in mei_nem Zir _ kel steh'n.
sicht, aus mei_nem Zir_kel bringt's mich nicht.
ein, es sei nicht Schan_de, klein zu sein.
klein, doch auch nicht kühn und ei _ tel sein.

12

"Sei du mein Trost"

K.391

Traurig, doch gelassen.
Mournful, yet calm.

Singstimme.

1. Sei_ du_ mein Trost, ver_schwieg_ne Trau_rig_keit! Ich flieh' zu
2. O_ Ein_sam_keit! wie sanft er_quickst du_ mich, wenn mei_ne
3. Hier wei_ne ich. Wie schmä_hend ist_ der_ Blick, mit dem ich
4. O_ dass_ dein Reiz, ge_lieb_te Ein_sam_keit! mir oft das

Pianoforte.

dir_ mit so viel Wun_den, nie klag' ich_ Glück_li_chen mein
Kräf_te früh er_mat_ten! Mit hei_sser Sehn_sucht such' ich
oft_ be_dau_ert wer_de! Jetzt, Thrä_nen, hält_ euch nichts zu_
Bild_ des Gra_bes bräch_te: so lockt des_ A_bends Dun_kel_

Leid: so schweigt ein Kran_ker bei Ge_sun_den.
dich:_ so sucht ein Wan_drer, matt, den Schat_ten.
rück: so senkt die Nacht Thau auf die Er_de.
heit_ zur tie_fen Ru_he. schö_ner Näch_te.

"Ich würd' auf meinem Pfad'"

K.390

Mässig, gehend.
Moderately, walking pace.

1. Ich würd' auf mei_nem Pfad'___ mit Thränen oft hin zum fer_nen
2. Den Son_nen_brand, der mich___ ent_kräftet, den Blitz, der mei_nem
3. Zwar schmerzt es mich, dass er___ den Jammer mit an_sieht und, zur
4. Dann brech' ich mu_thig durch___ die Dornen; „Er sieht mich blu_ten,"

En__de_ seh'n, säh' ich nicht Ken_ner mei__ner Lei_den so
Schei_tel_ droht, den sieht mein Freund und tritt mir nä_her und
Hälf_te_ schwach, nichts wei_ter kann, als mit mir trau_ern. Doch
sprech'_ ich_ dann. Und wenn ich einst, ver_blu__tet, fal_le, dann

mit_leids_voll am We_ge steh'n.
ruft: „Ich ken_ne dei_ne Noth."
ruft mein Herz: „Er weint dir nach."
sag' er: „Der stieg fel_sen_an."

14

Die Zufriedenheit

K.349

15

Die Zufriedenheit

K.349

(alternative setting with mandolin accompaniment)

Was frag' ich viel nach Geld und Gut, wenn ich zu _ frie _ den bin! Giebt Gott mir nur ge _ sun _ des Blut, so hab' ich fro _ hen Sinn, und sing' mit dank _ ba _ rem Ge _ müth mein Mor _ gen _ und mein A _ _ _ bend _ lied.

16

"Komm, liebe Zither"

K.351
(mandolin accompaniment)

(Lied zur) Gesellenreise

K.468

(organ accompaniment)

Die ihr ei _ nem neu _ en Gra _ de der Er _

kennt _ _ niss nun euch naht, _____ wan _ dert fest auf eu _ rem

Der Zauberer

K.472

1. Ihr Mäd _ chen, flieht Da _ mö _ ten
2. Sah ich ihn an, so ward mir
3. Er führ _ te mich in dies Ge _
4. Ent_brannt drückt' er mich an sein

ja! Als ich zum er_sten_mal ihn sah, da fühlt' ich,
heiss, bald ward ich roth, bald ward ich weiss, zu _ letzt nahm
sträuch, ich wollt' ihn flieh'n und folgt' ihm gleich; er setz _ _ te
Herz, was fühlt' ich! welch ein sü _ sser Schmerz! ich schluchzt', ich

so was fühlt' ich nie, mir ward,_____ mir ward, ich weiss nicht
er mich bei der Hand; wer sagt_____ mir, was ich da em-
sich, ich setz _ te mich; er sprach,_____ nur Syl _ ben stam-melt'
ath _ me _ te sehr schwer, da kam_____ zum Glück die Mut _ ter

sf

wie, ich seuf _ zte, zit _ ter _ te, und schien mich doch zu freu'n; glaubt mir, er
pfand? ich sah, ich hör _ te nichts, sprach nichts als Ja und Nein; glaubt mir, er
ich; die Au _ gen starr _ ten ihm, die mei _ nen wur _ den klein; glaubt mir, er
her; was würd', o Göt _ ter, sonst nach so viel Zau _ be _ rei'n, aus mir zu-

fp

muss ein Zaub' _ rer sein.
muss ein Zaub' _ rer sein.
muss ein Zaub' _ rer sein.
letzt ge _ wor _ den sein!

f

Die Zufriedenheit

K.473

sanft, wie ru_hig fühl' ich hier des Le_bens Freu_den oh_ne Sor _ gen! und

sehr lach' ich die Gro_ssen aus, die Blut_ver_gie_sser, Hel_den, Prin _ zen! denn

Die betrogene Welt

K.474

1. Der rei_che Thor, mit Gold ge_schmü_cket, zieht Se_li_
2. Be_a_te, die vor we_nig Ta_gen der Buh_le_
3. Wenn ich mein Ka_ro_lin_chen küs_se, schwör' ich ihr

me_nens Au_gen an;— der wack_re Mann wird fort_ge_schi_cket, den Stu_tzer
rin_nen Kro_ne war,— fängt an, sich vi_o_lett zu tra_gen und klei_det
zärt_lich ew'_ge Treu'; sie stellt sich, als ob sie nicht wis_se, dass au_sser

wählt sie sich zum Mann.
Kan - zel und Al - tar.
mir ein Jüng - ling sei.

Es wird ein
Dem äu - - - sser -
Einst, als mich

präch - tig Fest voll - zo - gen, bald hinkt die Reu - e hin - ter - drein, bald hinkt die
li - chen Schein ge - wo - gen, hält man - cher sie für en - gel - rein, hält man - cher
Chlo - e weg - ge - zo - gen, nahm mei - ne Stel - le Da - mis ein, nahm mei - ne

Reu - e hin - ter - drein.___ Die Welt will ja__ be - tro - gen sein, drum wer - de sie be - tro -
sie für en - gel - rein.___ Die Welt will ja__ be - tro - gen sein, drum wer - de sie be - tro -
Stel - le Da - mis ein.___ Soll al - le Welt be - tro - gen sein, so werd' auch ich be - tro -

gen, drum, drum wer - de sie be - tro - gen.
gen, drum, drum wer - de sie be - tro - gen.
gen, so, so werd' auch ich be - tro - gen.

Das Veilchen

K.476

Ein Veilchen auf der Wie_se stand, ge_bückt in sich und un_be_kannt: es war ein her_zig's Veil_

chen. Da kam ein' jun_ge Schä_fe_rin mit leich_tem Schritt und mun_term Sinn da_her, da_

her, die Wie_se her und sang.

Ach! denkt das Veil_chen,___ wär' ich nur die schön_ste Blu_me der Na_tur, ach, nur___

Lied der Freiheit

K.506

1. Wer un_ter ei_nes Mäd_chens Hand sich
2. Wer sich um Für_sten_gunst und Rang mit
3. Wer um ein schim_mern_des Me_tall dem
4. Doch wer dies al_les leicht ent_behrt, wo_

als ein Scla_ve schmiegt und, von der Lie_be fest_ge_bannt, in
sau_rem Schweiss be_müht,__ und, ein_ge_spannt sein Le_ben lang, am
bö_sen Mam_mon dient,__ und sei_ner vol_len Sä_cke Zahl nur
nach der Thor nur strebt,__ und froh bei sei_nem eig_nen Herd nur

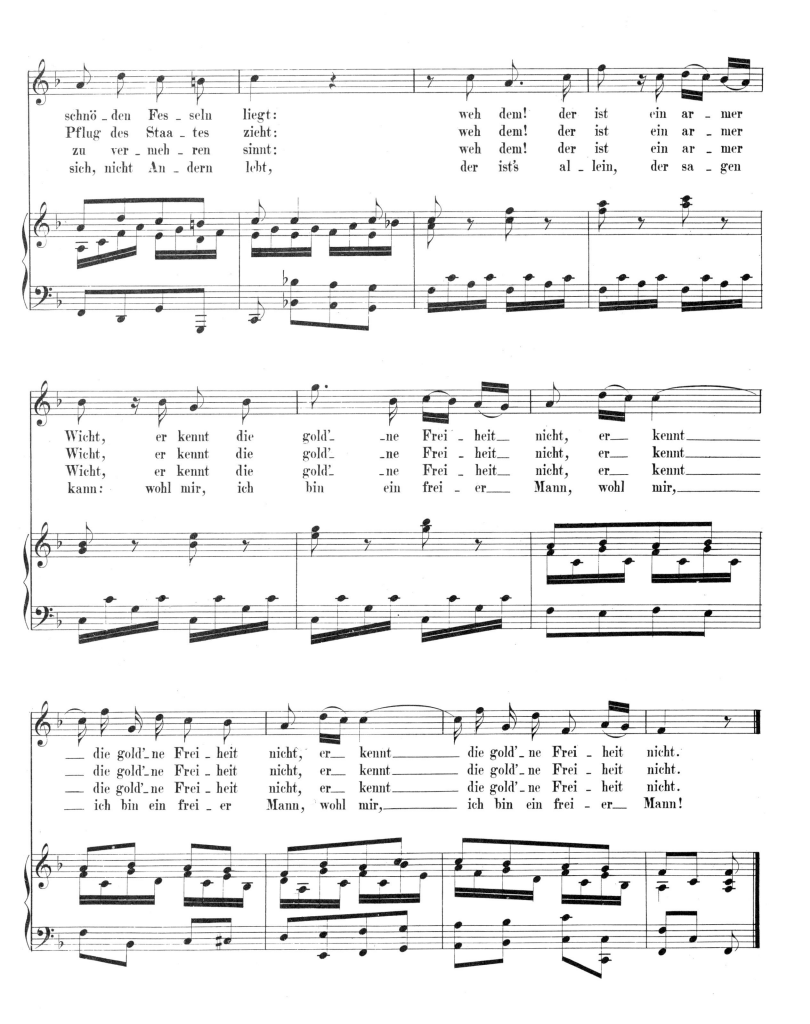

Die Alte

K.517

haf_ten__ Mäd_chen Bräu_te; doch al_les mit Be_schei_den_
dank_bar__ und ver_schwie_gen; doch jetzt ent_deckt er's un_ge_
lie_ben__ Frau re_gie_ret, trotz sei_ner stol_zen Männ_lich_
sprё_chen__ und uns hü_ten, wo man mit Freun_den sich er_

heit. O gu_te Zeit, o gu_te Zeit! Es ward kein Jüng_ling zum Ver_
scheut. O schlim_me Zeit, o schlim_me Zeit! Die Re_gung müt_ter_li_cher__
keit. O gu_te Zeit, o gu_te Zeit! Die From_me herrsch_te nur ge_
freut. O schlim_me Zeit, o schlim_me Zeit! Mit die_ser Neu_e_rung im

rä_ther, und uns_re Jung_fern frei_ten__ spä_ter, sie reiz_ten nicht der Müt_ter__
Trie_be, der Vor_witz und der Geist der__ Lie_be fährt jetzt oft schon in's Flü_gel_
lin_der, uns blieb der Hut und ihm die__ Kin_der; das war die Mo_de weit und
Lan_de, mit die_sem Fluch im E_he_stan_de hat ein Co_met uns längst be_

Neid. O gu_te Zeit, o gu_te Zeit!
kleid. O schlim_me Zeit, o schlim_me Zeit!
breit. O gu_te Zeit, o gu_te Zeit!
dräut. O schlim_me Zeit, o schlim_me Zeit!

Die Verschweigung

K.518

1. So _ _bald_ Da mö _ _tas Chlo _ _en sieht,_ so
2. Ver _ _misst_ er Chlo _ en auf der_ Flur, be _
3. Sie hat_ an Blu _ men ih _ _re_ Lust, er
4. Wenn sie_ ein küh _ ler, heit _ _rer_ Bach,_ be _

sucht_ er mit_ be _ red _ _ten Bli _ cken ihr sei _ ne Kla _ gen
trübt_ wird er_ von dan _ nen schei _ den; dann a _ _ber hüpft er
stil _ let täg _ lich ihr Ver _ lan _ gen; sie klo _ pfet schmei _ chelnd
schützt von Bü _ schen, ein _ ge _ la _ den, in sei _ nen Wel _ len

aus _ zu _ drü _ cken und _ ih _ re Wan _ ge glüht . Sie
vol _ ler Freu _ den, ent _ deckt er Chlo _ en _ nur. Er
ihm die Wan _ gen, und _ steckt sie an _ die _ Brust. Der
sich zu ba _ den, so _ schleicht er li _ stig nach. In

32

Das Lied der Trennung

K.519

Langsam.
Slow.

Singstimme.

1. Die En_gel Got _tes wei_nen, wo Lie_ben_de sich tren _ nen, wie
2. Im Wa_chen und im Trau_me werd' ich Lu _ i _ sa nen _ nen; den
3. Ich kann sie nicht ver_ges_sen, an al_len, al _ len En _ den ver_

Pianoforte.

werd' ich le _ ben können, o_ Mäd_chen, oh _ ne dich? Ein Fremdling al _ len Freuden, leb'
Na _ men zu be_kennen, sei_ Got_tes_dienst für mich; ihn nen_nen und ihn lo_ben werd'
folgt von ih _ ren Händen ein_Druck der Lie _ be mich. Ich zitt_re, sie zu fassen, und

ich fort_an dem Leiden. Und du? und du?_ Vielleicht auf e _ wig ver _ gisst Lu _ i _ sa
ich vor Gott noch dro_ben. Und du? und du?_ Vielleicht auf e _ wig ver _ gisst Lu _ i _ sa
fin _ de mich ver _ las_sen. Und du? und du?_ Vielleicht auf e_wig ver _ gisst Lu _ i _ sa

mich, vielleicht auf e_wig vergisst sie mich.
mich, vielleicht auf e_wig vergisst sie mich.
mich, vielleicht auf e_wig vergisst sie mich.

4. Ich kann sie nicht ver _ ges _ sen; dies Herz, von ihr ge _ schnit _ ten, scheint seuf _ zend mich zu

bit _ ten: „o___ Freund, ge _ denk' an mich!" Ach! dein will ich ge _ denken, bis sie ins Grab mich

sen _ ken. Und du? und du?__ Vielleicht auf e _ wig ver _ gisst Lu _ i _ sa mich, vielleicht auf

e _ wig vergisst sie mich. 5. Ver _ ges _ sen raubt in Stun _ den, was

Lie _ be jahr _ lang spen _ det. Wie ei _ ne Hand sich wen _ det, so wen _ den Her _ zen

sich. Wenn neu_e Hul_di_gun_gen mein Bild bei ihr ver_drun_gen, o Gott!

Vielleicht auf e_wig ver_gisst Lu_i_sa_mich. 6. Ach denk' an un_ser Scheiden, ach

denk' an un_ser Schei_den! Dies thränen_lo_se Schweigen, dies Auf_und Nie_der_stei_gen des

Her_zens drü_cke dich wie schweres Geister_scheinen, wirst du wen an_ders meinen, wirst

du mich einst ver_ges_sen, ver_ges_sen Gott und dich. 7. Ach denk' an un_ser Scheiden! Dies

37

Denk_mal,un _ ter Kü _ ssen auf mei _ nen Mund ge _ bis _ sen, das_ rich _ te mich und

dich! Dies Denkmal auf dem Munde, komm' ich zur Gei _ ster_stunde, mich war _ nend an _ zu_

zei _ gen, vergisst Lu _ i _ sa, Lu _ i _ _ _sa mich, komm' ich mich war _ nend an _ zu_

zei _ gen, vergisst Lu _ i _ sa, Lu _ i _ _ _sa mich, ver _ gisst sie

mich, ver _ gisst sie mich, ver _ gisst sie mich.

Als Luise die Briefe ihres ungetreuen Liebhabers verbrannte

K. 520

39

wie _ der, und all' die schwär _ me _ ri _ schen Lie _ der, denn ach! _

er sang nicht mir al _ _lein. Ihr bren _ _net nun, und

bald, ihr Lie _ ben, ist kei _ ne Spur von euch mehr hier.

cre _ _ _scen _ _ _do _ _al f p

Doch ach! der Mann, der euch ge _schrieben, brennt lan _ _ge _noch viel _

leicht _ in mir, brennt lan _ ge noch viel _ leicht in mir.

Abendempfindung an Laura

K.523

41

42

An Chloe

K.524

Her_zen klopft und glüht; und ich hal_te dich und küs_se dei_ne

Ro_sen_wan_gen warm, lie_bes Mäd_chen, und ich

schlie_sse zit_ternd dich in mei_nen Arm, in mei_nen Arm, in mei_nen Arm! Mädchen,

Mäd_chen und ich drü_cke dich___ an mei__nen Busen fest, der im

letz _ ten Au _ gen _ bli _ cke ster _ bend, ster _ _ bend nur _ dich

von _ sich lässt; den be _ rausch _ ten Blick um _ schattet ei _ ne dü _ stre Wol _ ke

mir, ei _ ne dü _ stre _ Wol _ ke _ mir, und ich si _ tze dann er _

mat _ tet, er _ mat _ tet, er _ mat _ tet, a _ _ ber se _ _ _ lig

ne - ben ___ dir, ___ er - mattet, er - mattet, er - mat_tet, a - ber ___

se ___ lig ne ___ ben dir, a - ber se - lig ne_ben dir, a - ber

se - lig ne_ben dir, ne - - ben dir, ___ ne - - ben

dir.

Des kleinen Friedrichs Geburtstag*

K.529

*) Unter dem kleinen Friedrich ist der damalige (1779) Erbprinz von Anhalt - Dessau gemeint.
*) This song celebrates the ninth birthday of Crown Prince Friedrich of Anhalt-Dessau, 27 December 1787.

sanft wie klei _ ne Schäf _ chen, und wie ein Täub _ chen mild.
Je _ dem, der es grüss _ te, gar freundlich Re _ de stehn.
rie _ fen All' und Je _ de: Der muss ge _ fei _ ert sein.
Al _ le, Al _ le san _ gen: Heil un _ serm Frie _ de _

1.2.3.

4.

rich! Und Gott im Him _ mel o _ ben er _

hör _ te ihr Ge _ bet. _____ Sein Se _ gen folgt dem Kna _ ben, da

wo er geht und steht.

Das Traumbild

K.530

Singstimme.

Pianoforte.

1. Wo bist du, Bild, das
2. Nun such' ich dich, mit
3. Komm sel ber, süsses
4. Dein grosses blau es

vor mir stand, als ich im Gar ten träum te, ins Haar den Ros ma
Harm er füllt, bald bei des Dor fes Lin den, bald in der Stadt, ge
Bild der Nacht, komm mit den En gel mie nen, und in der leich ten
Au gen paar, wo raus ein En gel blick te; die Stir ne, die so

rin mir wand, der um mein La ger keim te?
lieb tes Bild, und kann dich nir gends fin den.
Schä fer tracht, wo rin du mir er schie nen!
freundlich war, und gu ten A bend nick te;

Wo bist du, Bild, das vor mir stand, mir in die See _ le _
Nach je _ dem Fen _ ster blick' ich hin, wo nur ein Schlei _ er _
Bring' mit die schwa _ nen wei _ sse Hand, die mir das Herz _ ge _
den Mund, der Lie _ be Pa _ ra _ dies, die klei _ nen Wan _ gen _

blick _ te, und ei _ ne war _ me Mäd _ chen _ hand mir an die Wan _ gen
we _ het, und ha _ be mei _ ne Lieb _ lin _ gin noch nir _ gends aus _ ge _
stoh _ len, das pur _ pur _ ro _ the Bu _ sen _ band, das Sträuss _ chen von _ Vi _
grüb _ chen, wo sich der Him _ mel of _ fen wies: Bring' al _ les mit, _ mein

drück _ te?
spä _ het.
o _ len.
Lieb _ chen!

Die kleine Spinnerin

K.531

Sehnsucht nach dem Frühlinge

K.596

Fröhlich.
Joyfully.

Singstimme.

Pianoforte.

1. Komm, lie _ ber Mai, und ma _ che die Bäu _ me wie _ der grün, und lass mir an dem Ba _ che die
2. Zwar Win _ ter _ ta _ ge ha _ ben wohl auch der Freuden viel; man kann im Schnee eins tra _ ben und
3. Doch wenn die Vög _ lein sin _ gen und wir dann froh und flink auf grünen Ra _ sen springen, das
4. Am mei _ sten a _ ber dau _ ert mich Lottchens Her _ ze _ leid, das ar _ me Mäd _ chen lau _ ert recht
5. Ach wenn's doch erst ge _ lin _ der und grü _ ner draussen wär'! Komm, lie _ ber Mai, wir Kin _ der wir

klei _ nen Veilchen blühn! Wie möcht' ich doch so ger _ ne ein Veilchen wie _ der _ sehn, ach, lie _ ber Mai, wie
treibt manch A _ bend _ spiel, baut Häu _ ser _ chen von Kar _ ten, spielt Blinde _ kuh und Pfand; auch giebt's wohl Schlitten _
ist ein an _ der Ding! Jetzt muss mein Ste _ cken _ pferdchen dort in dem Win _ kel stehn; denn drau _ ssen in dem
auf die Blumen _ zeit; um _ sonst hol' ich ihr Spielchen zum Zeit _ ver _ treib her _ bei, sie sitzt in ih _ rem
bit _ ten dich gar sehr! O komm und bring vor Al _ len uns vie _ le Veil _ chen mit, bring' auch viel Nach _ ti _

ger _ ne ein _ mal spa _ zie _ ren gehn!
fahr _ ten auf's lie _ be frei _ e Land.
Gärt _ chen kann man vor Koth nicht gehn.
Stühlchen wie's Hühnchen auf dem Ei.
gal _ len und schö _ ne Gu _ kuks mit!

Im Frühlingsanfang

K.597

Etwas langsam.
Rather slow.

Singstimme.

Pianoforte.

1. Er _ wacht zum neu _ en Le _ ben steht vor mir die Na-
2. Die Flur im Blu _ men klei _ de ist, Schö _ pfer, dein Al-
3. O Va _ ter, dei _ ne Mil _ de fühlt Berg und Thal und
4. Ich schau' ihr nach und schwin _ ge voll Dank mich auf zu
5. Glänzt von der blau _ en Fe _ ste die Sonn' auf uns _ re
6. Lob _ sing' ihm, mei _ ne See _ le, dem Gott, der Freu _ den

tur,___ und sanf _ te Lüf _ te we _ hen durch die ver _ jüng _ te
tar,___ und O _ pfer rei _ ner Freu _ de weiht dir das jun _ ge
Au,___ es 'grü _ nen die Ge _ fil _ de, be _ perlt vom Mor _ gen-
dir,___ dem Schö _ pfer al _ ler Din _ ge, ge _ seg _ net seist___ du
Flur,_ so weiht zum Schö _ pfungs _ fe _ ste sich je _ de Kre _ a-
schafft! Lob _ sing' ihm und er _ zäh _ le die Wer _ ke sei _ ner

Flur. Em - por aus sei - ner Hül - le drängt sich der jun - ge
Jahr; es bringt die er - sten Düf - te der blau - en Veil - chen
thau; der Blu - men - weid' ent - ge - gen blökt schon die Herd' im
mir! Weit ü - ber sie er - ho - ben, kann ich der Flu - ren
tur, und al - le Blät - ter drin - gen aus ih - rem Keim her -
Kraft! Hier von dem Blü - then - hü - gel bis zu der Ster - ne
Halm, der Wäl - der ö - de Stil - le be - lebt der Vö - gel
dir, und schwe - bend durch die Lüf - te lob - singt die Ler - che
Thal, und in dem Stau - be re - gen sich Wür - mer oh - ne
Pracht em - pfin - den, kann dich lo - ben, der du den Lenz ge -
vor, und al - le Vö - gel schwin - gen sich aus dem Schlaf em -
Bahn steig' auf der An - dacht Flü - gel dein Lob - lied him - mel -
Psalm.
dir.
Zahl.
macht.
por.
an!
f
p

Das Kinderspiel

K.598

Munter.
Vigorous.

Singstimme.

Pianoforte.

mf

Wir Kin _ der, wir schme _ cken der Freu _ den recht viel, wir

schä _ kern und ne _ cken, ver _ steht sich im _ Spiel; wir lär _ men und

sin _ gen und ren _ nen rund _ um, und hü _ pfen und sprin _ gen im _

Gra _ se _ her _ um.

2.

Warum nicht? zum Murren
Ist's Zeit noch genug.
Wer wollte wohl knurren?
Der wär' ja nicht klug.
Wie lustig steh'n dorten
Die Saat und das Gras;
Beschreiben mit Worten
Kann Keiner wohl das.

3.

Ha! Brüderchen, rennet
Und wälzt euch im Gras!
Noch ist's uns vergönnet,
Noch kleidet uns das.
Ach, werden wir älter,
So schickt sich's nicht mehr,
Dann treten wir kälter
Und steifer einher.

4.

Ei, seht doch, ihr Brüder,
Den Schmetterling da!
Wer wirft ihn uns nieder?
Doch schonet ihn ja!
Dort flattert noch einer,
Der ist wohl sein Freund,
O schlag' ihn ja Keiner,
Weil jener sonst weint.

5.

Wird dort nicht gesungen?
Wie herrlich das klingt!
Vortrefflich, ihr Jungen,
Die Nachtigall singt.
Dort sitzt sie, dort oben
Im Apfelbaum, dort;
Wir wollen sie loben,
So fährt sie wohl fort.

6.

Komm Liebchen hernieder
Und lass' dich besch'n!
Wer lehrt dich die Lieder?
Du machst es recht schön!
O lass' dich nicht stören,
Du Vögelchen du!
Wir Alle, wir hören
So gerne dir zu.

7.

Wo ist sie geblieben?
Wir seh'n sie nicht mehr.
Da flattert sie drüben.
Komm wieder hier her!
Vergeblich, die Freude
Ist diesmal vorbei;
Ihr that wer zu Leide,
Sei, was es auch sei.

8.

Lasst Kränzchen uns winden,
Viel Blumen sind hier.
Wer Veilchen wird finden,
Empfängt was dafür.
Ein Mäulchen zur Gabe
Giebt Mutter, wohl zwei.
Juchheisa! ich habe,
Ich hab' eins, juchhei!

9.

Ach, geht sie schon unter,
Die Sonne, so früh?
Wir sind ja noch munter,
Ach, Sonne verzieh'!
Nun morgen, ihr Brüder,
Schlaft wohl, gute Nacht!
Ja, morgen wird wieder
Gespielt und gelacht.

Zur Eröffnung der

K.483

1. Zer _ flie _ sset heut', ge _ lieb _ te Brü _ der, in Wonn' und Ju _ bel _
2. Dank auch der Schaar, die eh uns wach _ te, der Tu _ gend Flamm' an _

lie _ der, Jo _ sephs Wohl _ thä _ _ tig _ keit hat uns, in de _ ren
fach _ te und uns zum Bei _ _ spiel war, aus de _ ren je _ dem

Brust ein drei _ fach Feu _ er brennt, hat un _ sre Hoff _ nung neu ge _
Tritt auf ih _ rem Mau _ rer _ gang ein Quell des Bru _ der _ wohls ent _

krönt. Ver _ ei _ ne _ ter Her _ zen und Zun _ _ gen sei
sprang. Das in _ nig _ ste, thä _ tig _ ste Stre _ _ ben, zu

Jo _ seph dies Lob _ lied ge _ sun _ _ gen, dem Va _ ter, der en _ ger uns

ih _ nen em _ por sich zu he _ _ ben, ist Al _ len der herr _ lich _ ste

band. __ Wohl _ thun ist die schön _ ste der Pflich _ ten; er

Dank. __ Drum lasst uns, ver _ drei _ facht die Kräf _ te, be _

sah sie uns feu _ rig ver _ rich _ ten und krönt uns mit lieb _ vol _ ler Hand, und

gin _ nen die ho _ hen Ge _ schäf _ te und schwei _ gen den fro _ hen Ge _ sang, und

krönt uns mit lieb _ vol _ ler Hand.

schwei _ gen den fro _ hen Ge _ sang.

Zum Schluss der ▭

K. 484

(voice, chorus, organ)

Andante.

Singstimme.

1. Ihr un_sre neu_en Lei_ter, nun dan_ken wir auch eu_rer
2. Hebt auf der Wahr_heit Schwin_gen uns hö_her zu der Weis_heit

Orgel.

Solo.

Treu_e; führt stets____ am Tu_gend_pfad uns wei_ter, dass
Thro_ne, dass wir____ ihr Hei__lig_thum er_rin_gen und

Je____der sich der Ket_te freu_e, die ihn an bess'_re Men_schen
wür__dig wer_den ih_rer Kro_ne, wenn ihr wohl_thä_tig für den

schliesst und ihm des Le_bens Kelch ver_süsst, und ihm____ des Le_bens
Neid Pro_fa_ner selbst durch uns ver_scheut, den Neid____ Pro_fa_ner

Das Bändchen

K.441

(trio)

62

64

68

"Grazie agl'inganni tuoi"

K.532

(trio)

Soprano. / Tenore. / Basso.

Gra_zie a_gl'in_gan_ni tuo_i, al fin re_spi_ro, o Ni_ce, al

fin d'un in_fe_li_ce eb_ber gli Dei pie_tà. Gra_zie a_gl'in_gan_ni tuo_i, al

fin d'un in_fe_li_ce eb_ber gli Dei pie_tà. Gra_zie, gra_zie!

72

E non t'of‿fen‿da il ve‿ro,___ e non t'of‿fen‿da il ve‿ro, nel tuo leg‿gia‿dro as‿pet‿to or

E non t'of‿fen‿da il ve‿ro, nel tuo leg‿gia‿dro as‿pet‿to or

Or sco‿pro al‿cun di‿ ‿ ‿fet‿to,

sco‿pro al‿cun di‿ ‿fet‿to, che mi pa‿rea bel‿ ‿tà.___ Gra‿zie a‿gl'in‿gan‿ni tuo‿i, al

sco‿pro al‿cun di‿ ‿fet‿to, che mi pa‿rea bel‿ ‿tà. Gra‿zie a‿gl'in‿gan‿ni tuo‿i, al

che mi pa‿ ‿rea bel‿ ‿tà. Gra‿zie a‿gl'in‿gan‿ni tuo‿i, al

fin re‿spi‿ro, o Ni‿ce, al fin d'un in‿fe‿ ‿li‿ ‿ce eb‿ber gli Dei pie‿ ‿tà. Gra‿zie a‿gl'in‿ganni

fin re‿spi‿ro, o Ni‿ce, al fin d'un in‿fe‿ ‿li‿ ‿ce eb‿ber gli Dei pie‿ ‿tà. Gra‿zie a‿gl'in‿ganni

fin re‿spi‿ro, o Ni‿ce, al fin d'un in‿fe‿ ‿li‿ ‿ce eb‿ber gli Dei pie‿ ‿tà. Gra‿zie a‿gl'in‿ganni

tuo‿i, al fin d'un in‿fe‿ ‿li‿ ‿ce eb‿ber gli Dei pie‿ ‿tà. Gra‿ ‿zie, gra‿ ‿zie!

tuo‿i, al fin d'un in‿fe‿ ‿li‿ ‿ce eb‿ber gli Dei pie‿ ‿tà. Gra‿ ‿zie, gra‿ ‿zie!

tuo‿i,___ al fin d'un in‿fe‿ ‿li‿ ‿ce eb‿ber gli Dei pie‿ ‿tà. Gra‿ ‿zie, gra‿ ‿zie!

"Un moto di gioja"

K.579

74

moto di gioja mi sento nel petto, che annunzia diletto in mezzo il ti-
klopfet mein liebender Busen vor Freuden, schon ahne ich bangend mein sel'ges Ge-

mor. Speriam che in contento finisca l'af-
schick. Bald wird sich in Wonne verwandeln mein

fanno, non sempre, non sempre è tiranno, non sempre è tiranno il
Leiden, nicht ewig, nicht ewig ist grausam, nicht ewig ist grausam die

fato ed amor, il fato ed amor, il fato ed a-
Lieb' und das Glück, die Lieb' und das Glück, die Lieb' und das

mor, il fato ed amor.
Glück, die Lieb' und das Glück.

Cantate
"Die ihr des unermesslichen Weltalls"
K.619

75

Brüder, liebt euch selbst und eu _ re Brü _ _ _ der,

und eu _ re Brü _ _ der! Kör _ per_kraft und Schön _ heit

sei eu _ re Zierd', Ver _ stan _ _ _ des_hel _ le eu _ _ er

A _ del! Reicht euch der ew'_ _ gen Freund _ schaft Bruderhand, die nur ein

Wahn, nie Wahrheit, euch____ so lang ent _ zog, die nur ein

78

Ei_sen, das Men_schen_, das Brü_der_ _blut bis_her ver-

goss!

Zerspren_get Fel_ _sen mit dem schwarzen

Stau_be, der mor_dend Blei_____ in's Bruderherz oft schnellte!

Recitativ.

Andante.

Wähnt nicht, dass wah_res Un_glück sei auf mei_ner Er_ _de! Be_

lehrung ist es nur, die wohl_thut, wenn sie euch zu bes_ _sern Tha_ten spornt, die,

Men _ schen, ihr in Un _ glück wan _ delt, wenn thö _ richt blind ihr rück _ wärts in den

Recitativ.

Sta _ _ chel schlagt, der vor _ wärts, vor _ wärts euch an _ trei _ ben

Andante, a tempo.

soll _ te. Seid wei _ se nur, seid kraftvoll, und _____ seid Brü _ der!

Dann ruht auf euch mein ganzes Wohlge _ fal _ len, dann ne _ tzen Freu _ denzähren nur die

Wan _ gen, dann wer _ den eu _ re Klagen Jubel _ tö _ ne, dann schaf _ fet

"Daphne, deine Rosenwangen"

K.52

(arr. by Leopold Mozart of an aria from *Bastien und Bastienne*)

Die grossmüthige Gelassenheit

K.149

(Leopold Mozart)

Geheime Liebe

K.150

(anon.)

Im Tempo eines gewissen geheimen Vergnügens.
In the tempo of a certain secret pleasure.

Was ich in Ge _ dan _ ken kü _ sse, ma _ _ _ chet

mir das _ Le _ ben _ sü _ sse und ver _ treibt so

Gram als Zeit. Nie _ mand soll es auch er _ _ fah _ ren,

nie _ mand will ich's of _ fen _ ba _ ren, als der stum _ men

Ein _ sam _ keit, als der stum _ men Ein _ sam _ keit.

Die Zufriedenheit im niedrigen Stande

K.151

(anon.)

Ich trach_te nicht nach sol _ chen Din _ gen, die hoch und zu ge _ fähr _ lich sind; mein Geist sucht nir _ _ _ gends durch_zu_ drin _ gen, als wo er leich _ te Bah _ ne findt. Ich ru_he sanft bis an den Mor_gen, wenn Mancher, wel _ cher vol_ler Sor _ gen nach eit_ler Hoff _ nung ängst_lich ringt, der blin_den Göt _ _ tin Weih_rauch bringt. Ich ru _ he bringt.

Canzonetta
"Ridente la calma"
K.152
(arr. by Mozart of the aria "Il caro mio bene" by Josef Mysliveček)

Wiegenlied

K.350

(Bernhard Flies)

1. Schlafe, mein Prinzchen, es ruh'n Schäfchen und Vö_gel_chen nun,
2. Al_les im Schlos_se schon liegt, Al_les in Schlummer ge_wiegt;
3. Wer ist be_glück_ter als du? Nichts als Ver_gnü_gen und Ruh',

Gar_ten und Wie_se verstummt, auch nicht ein Bienchen mehr summt, Lu_na mit sil_ber_nem
re_get kein Mäuschen sich mehr, Kel_ler und Kü_che sind leer, nur in der Zo_fe Ge_
Spielwerk und Zu_cker voll_auf, und noch Ka_ros_sen im Lauf, Al_les be_sorgt und be_

Schein gu_cket zum Fen_ster her_ein. Schlafe beim sil_ber_nen Schein,
mach tö_net ein schmachten_des Ach. Was für ein Ach mag dies sein?
reit, dass nur mein Prinzchen nicht schreit. Was wird da künftig erst sein?

schlafe, mein Prinzchen, schlaf' ein, schlaf' ein, _____ schlaf' ein!
Schlafe, mein Prinzchen, schlaf' ein, schlaf' ein, _____ schlaf' ein!
Schlafe, mein Prinzchen, schlaf' ein, schlaf' ein, _____ schlaf' ein!

TRANSLATIONS OF THE TEXTS

An die Freude (To Joy; text by Johann Peter Uz, 1720–1796)

1. Joy, queen of wise men,
   Who, with flowers circling their heads,
   Praise you on golden lyres,
   Calm while malice is raging:
   Hear me from your throne,
   Child of Wisdom, whose hand
   Has always bound her fairest roses
   In your crown herself.

2. Roses that with fresh petals
   Blossom immortally in spite of the north wind,
   In spite of the south wind, in the midst of storms,
   When the clouds emit flames,
   Roses that twine through your wavy hair,
   Not only on Cytherea's [Venus'] breast,
   When the Graces sing to you,
   Or during Lyaeus' [Bacchus'] pleasure.

3. They wreathe you at times
   That no glance of the sun illuminates,
   They saw you combating prosperity,
   The tyrant of our world,
   Who drew thundering clouds
   Around his gigantic limbs
   And with frightful plumage
   Flew between earth and sky.

4. You and your roses were also seen
   By the realms of night
   As you approached the throne of death,
   Where cold fear keeps vigil.
   Your path, where you walked,
   Was marked by the gentle light
   Of Cynthia [the moon] with her full cheeks,
   Which breaks through dark shadows.

5. This lord of life,
   Death, was not fearsome to you,
   And in vain did he brandish
   His javelin against you:
   Because in that sad region
   Hope walked beside you
   And with her shield of adamant
   Hovered over your head.

6. If I have taught my bold strings
   Resounding praise of you,
   Which perhaps in remote ages
   Our as yet unborn descendants shall hear;
   If I have investigated the flowery paths
   On which you walk,
   And from stormy shores
   Have led some people to you:

7. Then, Goddess, I beseech you, be
   Always favorable to your poet,
   That he may spurn the glitter of prosperity,
   Rich in himself even without gold;
   That his life may be obscure perhaps
   But without slavery,
   Without blemishes, without cares,
   And dear to wise friends!

Wie unglücklich bin ich nit (How Unhappy I Am; text anon.)

How unhappy I am,
How languishing are my steps,
When I wend my way to you.
Only my sighs comfort me,
All sorrows accumulate,
When I think of you.

O heiliges Band (O Holy Bond; text by Ludwig Friedrich Lenz, 1717–1780)

O holy bond of friendship's loyal brothers,
Like the highest happiness and Eden's bliss,
Friendly to religion, but never set against
The world, well known and yet full of mystery.

Oiseaux, si tous les ans (Birds, If Every Year; French text by Antoine Ferrand, 1678–1719, and German translation by Daniel Jäger)

FRENCH:
Birds, if every year you fly to another region
As soon as sad winter despoils our forests,
It is not merely to find fresh leafy trees,
Nor to avoid our chills.

94

But your destiny
Does not allow you to love unless flowers are in season.
And when that season is past,
You seek it elsewhere,
So that you can love all year long.

GERMAN:

Of course you birds change
Your grove yearly
And, when cold winds blow,
You seek a warmer climate.
But the cause is not solely
The weather and the grove
If you enjoy this change.
Fate does not grant you
The happiness of love
Except in the time of blossoms
When that time [2ª volta: springtime] is finished here,
You search out another location for it,
And thus you love year in, year out.

Dans un bois (In a Wood; French text by Antoine Houdart de la Motte, 1672–1731, and German translation by Daniel Jäger)

FRENCH:

In a wood lonely and dark
I was strolling the other day;
A child was sleeping in the shade there;
It was fearsome Cupid.
I approached, charmed by his beauty,
But I should have been wary of him;
He had the features of an ungrateful woman
Whom I had sworn to forget.
His lips were as red,
His complexion as rosy as hers;
A sigh escaped me, he awoke—
Love is awakened by the slightest things.
Immediately unfurling his wings
And seizing his revenging bow,
[With] one of his cruel arrows
He wounded me in the heart as he left.
"Go," he said, "to languish
And burn again at Sylvia's feet!
You will love her all your life
Because you dared to awaken me."

GERMAN:

Recently I was walking alone in the grove
When I noticed in the bushes
A boy who had fallen asleep.
Ah! it was the malicious Cupid.
How lovely and friendly he seemed lying there!
But my heart could not trust him,
For he resembled the ungrateful woman
Whom I had sworn to forget.
I found his lips so fiery,
His face so fresh and fair,
And an "Ah!" escaped me; he awoke.
Ah! Love awakens even unaroused.
Suddenly his wings stirred,
He bent his revenging bow;
One of his bloodstained arrows
He seized and pierced my heart deeply.
"Away!" he called, "to Sylvia's feet!

Once more feel heart's pain and burning!
Now you shall love her as long as you live;
This is your punishment for awakening me."

Verdankt sei es dem Glanz (I Thank the Glory; text from the novel *Sophiens Reise* [*Sophie's Journey*] by Johann Timotheus Hermes, 1738–1821)

1. I thank the glory of the great
   For showing me my insignificance so clearly.
   It has never repulsed me
   Because it has never reached me.
   I saw many small men going nearer
   And I remained within my bounds.

2. I value them, the narrow boundaries
   In which I am so inconsiderable.
   Here I see medals and decorations shining,
   And I do not long for the ribbon or the star.
   And even the most gracious face
   Does not make me leave my bounds.

3. If the bad temper of a nobleman shows me
   That I am just a nonentity,
   Then, Innocence, teach me to be silent
   And give me fearlessness,
   And impress upon me with gentle consolation
   That it is no shame to be small.

4. But if some great man should, without hypocrisy,
   Descend to my level,
   Then, Experience, make me wise
   And delineate my boundaries,
   And teach me never to be too small
   But also neither bold nor vain.

Sei du mein Trost (Be My Comfort; text from *Sophie's Journey* by Johann Timotheus Hermes)

1. Be my comfort, discreet sadness!
   I flee to you with so many wounds;
   I shall never complain of my sorrows to happy people:
   Thus a sick person is silent in the company of the healthy.

2. O solitude! how gently you refresh me
   When my strength fails me prematurely!
   With hot longing I seek you:
   Thus a wayfarer, weary, seeks the shade.

3. Here I weep. How contemptuous is the glance
   With which I am often pitied!
   Now, tears, nothing keeps you back:
   Thus night lets dew fall on the earth.

4. O, may your charms, beloved solitude,
   Often bring me the image of the grave:
   Thus the darkness of evening lures one
   To the deep repose of beautiful nights.

Ich würd' auf meinem Pfad' (On My Path I Would; text from *Sophie's Journey* by Johann Timotheus Hermes)

1. On my path I would, with tears,
   Often look toward the distant end
   If I did not see people acquainted with my sorrows
   Standing along the way so sympathetically.

2. The sun's heat that weakens me,
   The lightning that threatens my head,
   My friend sees them and steps nearer to me
   And calls: "I know your distress."

3. To be sure, it pains me that he also sees
   My distress and, in his partial weakness,
   Can do no more than grieve with me.
   But my heart calls: "He weeps for you."

4. Then I break courageously through the thorns;
   "He sees me bleeding," I then say.
   And when, some day, I fall from loss of blood,
   Then let him say: "He climbed uphill."

Die Zufriedenheit (Contentment; text by Johann Martin Miller, 1750–1814)

1. Why should I ask much for money and property,
   If I am contented?
   If only God gives me good health,
   My mind is happy,
   And with grateful spirit I sing
   My morning and my evening song.

2. So many people have more than they need,
   House and estate and money,
   And yet are always full of vexation,
   And don't enjoy the world.
   The more they have, the more they want,
   Their complaints never end.

3. Then they call the world a vale of tears,
   Although I find it so beautiful;
   It has joys without measure and number,
   It sends no one away empty-handed.
   The little beetle, the little bird
   Can also enjoy the springtime.

4. And for our sake are adorned
   The meadow, hill and forest;
   And birds sing far and near,
   Making everything resound;
   When we work the lark sings to us,
   The nightingale during our sweet repose.

5. And when the golden sun rises,
   And the world becomes golden,
   And everything is blossoming,
   And the field bears ears of grain,
   Then I think: All this splendor
   Was created by God for my pleasure.

6. Then I praise God and laud God
   And my spirits soar,
   And I think: God is kind
   And wishes people well.
   Therefore I shall always be grateful
   And enjoy God's goodness.

Komm, liebe Zither (Come, Dear Zither; text anon.)

1. Come, dear zither, come, you friend of silent love,
   You shall be my friend as well.
   Come, to you I confide the most secret of my urges,
   Only to you I confide my sorrow.

2. Tell her for me, for I may not tell her yet,
   That my heart belongs completely to her.
   Tell her for me, for I may not lament to her yet,
   How my heart is consumed for her.

(Lied zur) Gesellenreise ([Song for] Journeyman's Travels; text by Josef Franz von Ratschky, 1757–1810)

You who are now approaching
A new level of knowledge,
Walk securely on your path,
Know that it is the path of wisdom.
Only a man who is persevering
May approach the source of light.

Der Zauberer (The Sorcerer; text by Christian Felix Weisse, 1726–1804)

1. Girls, shun Damoetas!
   When I first saw him,
   I felt—I never felt anything like it—
   I don't know what—what came over me—
   I sighed, trembled and yet seemed happy;
   Believe me, he must be a sorcerer!

2. If I looked at him I got hot,
   Now I turned red, now I turned white;
   Finally he took me by the hand;
   Who can say what my feelings were then?
   I saw and heard nothing, said nothing but yes and no;
   Believe me, he must be a sorcerer!

3. He led me into these bushes,
   I wanted to run from him and yet followed him at once;
   He sat down, I sat down;
   He spoke, I merely stammered syllables;
   His eyes were bulging, mine narrowed;
   Believe me, he must be a sorcerer!

4. He ardently pressed me to his heart;
   How I felt! what a sweet pain!
   I sobbed, I breathed very heavily,
   Then luckily my mother came by;
   O gods, after so much sorcery,
   What would finally have become of me!

Die Zufriedenheit (Contentment; text by Christian Felix Weisse)

1. How gentle, how calm I here feel
   Life's joys without cares!
   And without foreboding every morning
   Is welcome as it lights my way.
   My happy, my contented heart
   Dances to the melody of the groves
   And even my sorrow is pleasant
   When I weep for love.

2. How I deride the men of substance,
   The shedders of blood, heroes, princes!
   For a small house makes me happy,
   While they are not even satisfied with provinces.
   How they rage among themselves,
   The godlike masters of the earth!
   But do they need more room than I
   When they are buried?

Die betrogene Welt (The Deceived World; text by Christian Felix Weisse)

1. A rich fool, adorned with gold,
   Attracts Selimena's eyes;
   A stouthearted man is sent packing,
   And she chooses the dandy for her husband.
   A splendid celebration is held;
   Soon repentance limps by, too late.
   The world wishes to be deceived,
   And so let it be deceived.

2. Beata, who a few days ago
   Was the paragon of wanton women,
   Begins to dress in violet
   And frequents pulpits and altars.
   Relying on outward appearances,
   Many people consider her chaste as an angel.
   The world wishes to be deceived,
   And so let it be deceived.

3. When I kiss my dear Caroline,
   I tenderly swear to be eternally faithful to her;
   She acts as if she didn't know
   That any boy existed except me.
   Once, when Chloe had lured me away,
   Damis took my place.
   If the whole world is to be deceived,
   Then let me be deceived as well.

Das Veilchen (The Violet; text by Johann Wolfgang von Goethe, 1749–1832)

A violet stood in the meadow,
Withdrawn and unknown;
It was a charming violet.
There came a young shepherdess
With light tread and cheerful mind
Walking in the meadow and singing.
"Ah," the violet thinks, "if I only were
The loveliest flower in nature,
Ah, just for a little while,
Until my darling has picked me
And crushed me to death on her bosom,
Ah, only for a quarter of an hour!"
Ah, but alas! the girl came
And didn't even notice the violet,
She stepped on the poor violet.
It sank and died, and yet was happy:
"Even if I am dying, I am still dying
Because of her, and at her feet."
(The poor violet! It was a charming violet.)

Lied der Freiheit (Song of Liberty; text by Johannes Aloys Blumauer, 1755–1798)

1. The man who, like a slave, cringes
   Under a girl's thumb
   And, spellbound by love,
   Lies in vile fetters:
   Alas for him! he is a poor wretch,
   He has no knowledge of golden liberty.

2. The man who, with bitter toil, strives
   For rank and the favor of princes

And, in harness all his life,
Pulls the plow of the state:
Alas for him! he is a poor wretch,
He has no knowledge of golden liberty.

3. The man who, for the sake of gleaming metal,
   Serves evil Mammon
   And thinks only of increasing
   The number of his full moneybags:
   Alas for him! he is a poor wretch,
   He has no knowledge of golden liberty.

4. But the man who readily does without all
   That the fool yearns for
   And, happy at his own hearth,
   Lives only for himself, not for others,
   It is he alone who can say:
   Good for me, I am a free man!

Die Alte (The Old Woman; text by Friedrich von Hagedorn, 1708–1754)

1. In my day, in my day,
   Proper and reasonable ways still had currency.
   Then, too, children became solid citizens
   And virtuous girls became brides;
   But all with modesty.
   Oh, the good days, the good days!
   No young fellow deceived his sweetheart,
   And our maidens courted later,
   They didn't provoke their mothers' jealousy.
   Oh, the good days, the good days!

2. In my day, in my day,
   People were careful to be discreet.
   If a young man enjoyed a pleasure,
   He was grateful and kept still;
   But now he reveals it unabashedly.
   Oh, the bad times, the bad times!
   The stirring of maternal urges,
   Inquisitiveness and the spirit of love
   Are nowadays already found beneath pinafores!
   Oh, the bad times, the bad times!

3. In my day, in my day,
   Duty and order were not profaned.
   A man, as is fitting,
   Was ruled by a loving wife,
   Despite his proud virility.
   Oh, the good days, the good days!
   The pious woman merely governed more gently,
   We were left with the hat [the upper hand] and he with the children;
   That was the fashion far and wide.
   Oh, the good days, the good days!

4. In my day, in my day,
   There was still unity in marriages.
   Nowadays the husband can practically order us around,
   Contradict us and guard us
   When we are having a good time with friends.
   Oh, the bad times, the bad times!
   With this novelty in the land,
   With this curse on matrimony,
   We were long threatened by a comet.
   Oh, the bad times, the bad times!

Die Verschweigung (The Concealment; text by Christian Felix Weisse)

1. As soon as Damoetas sees Chloe,
   He attempts with eloquent glances
   To express his laments to her,
   And her cheeks glow.
   She seems to more-than-half understand
   His silent laments,
   And he is young, and she is beautiful:
   I shall say no more.

2. If he fails to meet Chloe in the meadow,
   He will depart from there sadly;
   But then he skips, full of joy,
   If only he discovers Chloe.
   With a thousand questions he kisses
   Her hand, and Chloe offers no resistance,
   And he is young, and she is beautiful:
   I shall say no more.

3. She takes pleasure in flowers,
   He gratifies her desire daily;
   She flatteringly taps him on the cheeks,
   And places them on her breast.
   Her bosom swells to wear them.
   He triumphs to see them there,
   And he is young, and she is beautiful:
   I shall say no more.

4. When a cool, merry brook,
   Protected by bushes, has invited her
   To bathe in its waves,
   He cunningly steals after her.
   On these sultry summer days
   He has often watched her,
   And he is young, and she is beautiful:
   I shall say no more.

Das Lied der Trennung (The Song of Separation; text by Klamer Eberhard Karl Schmidt, 1746–1824)

1. God's angels weep when lovers part;
   How can I go on living,
   Maiden, without you?
   A stranger to all joys,
   I live henceforth for sorrow.
   And you? And you? Perhaps Luisa will forget me forever,
     perhaps she will forget me forever.

2. Waking and dreaming I will speak Luisa's name;
   Let the acknowledgment of her name
   Be a divine service for me;
   I shall still speak it and praise it
   When standing before God up above.
   And you? [. . .] forget me forever.

3. I cannot forget her; every-, everywhere
   A pressure of love
   From her hands pursues me.
   I tremble to take hold of her
   And find myself abandoned.
   And you? [. . .] forget me forever.

4. I cannot forget her; my heart, cut by her,
   Seems to ask for me with sighs:

"O friend, remember me!"
Ah! I will remember *you*
Until they lower me into the grave.
And you? [. . .] forget me forever.

5. Oblivion steals in hours what love grants over years.
   As a hand turns,
   So hearts change.
   When new attentions paid to her
   Have suppressed my image in her mind,
   O God! Perhaps Luisa will forget me forever.

6. Ah, think of our parting, ah, think of our parting!
   May this tearless silence,
   May this rising and falling
   Of the heart oppress you
   Like the baleful apparition of ghosts
   If you ever love someone else,
   If you ever forget me, forget God and yourself.

7. Ah, think of our parting! Let this memorial,
   Bitten into my lips while we kissed,
   Judge you and me!
   With this memorial on my lips
   I shall come at the witching hour
   To present myself with a warning
   If Luisa forgets me, if she forgets me.

Als Luise die Briefe ihres ungetreuen Liebhabers verbrannte (When Luise Burned the Letters of her Faithless Lover; text by Gabriele von Baumberg, 1766–1839)

Begotten of a heated imagination,
Born in a visionary hour,
Perish,
You children of melancholy!
You owe your being to flames,
Now I restore you to the flames,
Along with all the fanciful songs,
For, alas! he sang not for me alone.
Now you are burning, and soon, dear ones,
No trace of you will remain.
But, ah! the man who wrote you
May still burn within me for a long time.

Abendempfindung an Laura (Evening Feelings for Laura; text perhaps by Joachim Heinrich Campe, 1746–1818)

It is evening, the sun has disappeared
And the moon beams with a silvery glow;
Thus life's fairest hours slip away,
Hasten by as if in a dance.
Soon life's variegated scene slips away
And the curtain rolls down;
Our play is over, our friends' tears
Already flow onto our grave.
Soon perhaps—a quiet premonition,
Soft as a westerly breeze, wafts toward me—
I shall terminate the pilgrimage of this life
And fly to the land of repose.
When you weep then by my grave,
And sadly look at my ashes,
Then, friends, I will appear to you
And will send you heavenly breezes.
[ADDRESSING ONE PERSON:]

Spare me a tear also, and pick
A violet for my grave,
And with your soulful gaze
Look down at me gently.
Dedicate a tear to me and, oh, do not
Be ashamed to dedicate it to me;
Oh, then in my diadem
It will be the most beautiful pearl.

An Chloe (To Chloe; text by Johann Georg Jacobi, 1740–1814)

When Love peers out from your blue,
Bright open eyes,
And my heart pounds and glows
With the pleasure of looking into them;
And I hold you and kiss
Your warm, rosy cheeks,
Dear girl, and I enfold
You tremblingly in my arms;
My girl, my girl, and I press
You tightly to my bosom,
Which will only give you up
At the last moment of death;
A dark cloud shades
My intoxicated eyes,
And I then sit, exhausted
But blissful, next to you.

Des kleinen Friedrichs Geburtstag (Little Friedrich's Birthday; text by Johann Eberhard Friedrich Schall, 1742–1790, from Joachim Heinrich Campe's *Kinderbibliothek* [Children's Library])

1. Once upon a time, little people, there was a young, gentle little boy,
   Named Friedrich, who was also of a very kind disposition.
   He was friendly and modest, not delicate and not wild,
   Was as gentle as little sheep and as mild as a little dove.

2. Thus God granted him vigor, and the little boy grew up,
   And his parents were very happy with him.
   He was seen going diligently to school and church,
   And conversing in a very friendly way with all who greeted him.

3. Also, in school everyone was greatly fond of him,
   For he made everyone happy and was kind to everyone.
   Once, the word came: "Brothers, tomorrow is his birthday!"
   Immediately one and all shouted: "It must be celebrated!"

4. Then there was much pleasure and all kinds of joy,
   And wherever one looked and listened, there was song and dance
      and sport,
   For everyone, everyone rejoiced in the happy day,
   And everyone, everyone sang: "Health to our Friedrich!"
   And God in heaven above granted their prayer.
   His blessing follows the boy wherever he goes or stays.

Das Traumbild (The Dream Vision; text by Ludwig Heinrich Christoph Hölty, 1748–1776)

1. Where are you, image that stood before me
   When I dreamt in the garden,
   That twined rosemary in my hair,
   That budded around my couch?
   Where are you, image that stood before me,
   Gazed into my soul,

And pressed a girl's warm hand
Against my cheeks?

2. Now I seek you, filled with sorrow,
   Now near the village lime trees,
   Now in the city, beloved image,
   And can find you nowhere.
   I look toward every window
   Where a veil flutters,
   But I have not yet anywhere
   Espied my darling.

3. Come yourself, sweet image of the night,
   Come with your angelic looks,
   And in the light shepherdess' garment
   In which you appeared to me!
   Bring along your swan-white hand,
   Which has stolen my heart,
   Your red-purple breastband,
   The little bouquet of violets;

4. Your two big blue eyes,
   From which an angel peered;
   Your brow, which was so friendly,
   And nodded good evening;
   Your lips, the paradise of love,
   The little dimples in your cheeks
   In which heaven displayed itself openly:
   Bring everything along, my darling!

Die kleine Spinnerin (The Little Spinner; original text anon.; stanzas 2 & 3 added by Daniel Jäger)

1. "What are you spinning?" asked Fritz, the neighbors' boy,
   When he visited us recently;
   "Your wheel is turning like lightning;
   Tell me what's the good of it;
   Instead, come and join our game!"
   "Mr. Fritz, I will not join in;
   If you must know, I can
   Pass the time this way, too!"

2. "What would I get from you, sirs?
   We know your ways, after all:
   You tease and joke and like to dance
   Round and round with girls;
   You heat your blood and make your feelings
   Active in every vein;
   You play the game as merrily as you can
   And then go your ways."

3. "It's almost as if girls existed
   Merely as playthings.
   So go and play wherever you like,
   I appreciate my spinning wheel.
   If I am to spin silk,
   Then—pay heed, Mr. Fritz—
   I don't want to get tow while at it."

Sehnsucht nach dem Frühlinge (Longing for Springtime; text by Christian Adolf Overbeck, 1755–1821)

1. Come, dear May, and make
   The trees green again,
   And let the little violets
   Bloom by the brook for me!
   How I would like

To see a violet again,
Ah, dear May, how gladly
I would go for a stroll!

2. To be sure, winter days have
Many joys also;
You can take a walk in the snow
And play many games in the evening,
Build houses of cards,
Play blindman's buff and forfeits;
There are also sleighrides
Into the dear open countryside.

3. But when the birds sing
And we then merrily and nimbly
Leap on green lawns,
That is something else again!
Now my hobbyhorse
Must stand in the corner there;
For outside in the little garden
It is impossible to go because of the mud.

4. But I feel sorriest for
Little Lotte's sadness;
The poor girl is really looking forward
To blossom time;
In vain I bring her games
To pass the time,
She sits on her little chair
Like a hen on its eggs.

5. Ah, if it were only milder
And greener outside!
Come, dear May, we children
Beg you so!
Oh, come, and above all bring
Along many violets for us,
Also bring many nightingales
And lovely cuckoos along!

Im Frühlingsanfang (At the Beginning of Spring; text by Christoph Christian Sturm, 1740–1786)

1. Awakened to new life,
Nature stands before me,
And gentle breezes blow
Through the rejuvenated fields.
The young blade of grass
Pushes up out of its sheath,
The barren silence of the forests
Is enlivened by the birds' psalm.

2. The fields in their garment of flowers
Are Your altar, Creator,
And the young year consecrates
Offerings of pure joy to You;
It brings You the first fragrances
Of the blue violets,
And, soaring through the skies,
The lark sings Your praises.

3. O Father, Your kindness
Fills mountain, valley and meadow;
The fields grow green,
Spangled with morning dew;
The flock in the valley already bleats
As it approaches the flowery pasture,

And in the dust
Worms without number stir.

4. I follow it* with my eyes and,
Full of gratitude, rise up to You in spirit,
To You, Creator of all things—
Blessing upon You!
Raised far above them,
I can feel the glory of the fields,
I can praise You,
You who made the springtime.

5. When from its blue fortress
The sun shines upon our fields,
Every created thing devotes itself
To the celebration of creation,
And all the leaves push
Out of their buds,
And all the birds rise up
Out of sleep.

6. Sing His praises, my soul,
The praises of God, who creates joys!
Sing His praises and tell
The results of His power!
Here from the blossoming hill
Up to the path of the stars,
Let your song of praise climb heavenward
On the wings of piety!

*The "it" seems to refer to the lark in the last line of stanza 2, indicating that the stanza numbered 4 here is out of place.

Das Kinderspiel (Children's Games; text by Christian Adolf Overbeck)

1. We children taste
Many joys,
We joke and tease,
But only in play, of course;
We make noise and sing
And run around,
And hop and jump
Around in the grass.

2. Why not? For grumbling
There's time enough.
Who wants to snarl?
Whoever does isn't smart.
How merrily they stand there,
The grainfields and the grass;
I'm sure nobody can
Describe them in words.

3. Ha! Brothers, run
And roll in the grass!
It is still granted us to do so,
It still becomes us.
Ah, when we grow older,
It will no longer be proper,
Then we will walk around
More coldly and stiffly.

4. Oh, brothers, look
At the butterfly there!
Who'll knock it down?
But spare it!
There flutters another one,

It's surely his friend;
Let nobody hit it,
Or the other one will cry.

5. Isn't someone singing there?
How splendid it sounds!
Excellently, boys,
The nightingale sings.
There it sits, up there
In the apple tree there;
We will praise it,
And so it will probably continue.

6. Come down, dear,
And let us see you!
Who teaches you your songs?
You sing them really beautifully!
Oh; don't let us disturb you,
Little bird!
We all like so much
To listen to you.

7. Where did it go?
We don't see it any more.
There it is, fluttering over there.
Come back here!
No use, this time
The pleasure is over;
Somebody did it some harm
Of whatever sort.

8. Let's twine wreaths,
There are many flowers here.
Whoever finds violets
Will get something for it.
Mother will give you a kiss
As a gift, maybe two.
Hurray! I have it,
I have one, hurray!

9. Ah, is it going down already,
The sun, so early?
We're still lively;
Ah, sun, delay!
Well, tomorrow, brothers—
Sleep well, good night!—
Yes, tomorrow once more
There will be games and laughter.

Zur Eröffnung der ☐ (For the Inauguration of ☐;
text by Augustin Veith von Schlittersberg, 1751–1811)

1. Pour yourselves forth today,
Beloved brothers,
In songs of rapture and jubilation;
[Emperor] Joseph's beneficence
Has for us, in whose breast a triple fire burns,
Newly crowned our hopes.
CHORUS: With united hearts and tongues
Let this song of praise be sung to Joseph,
To the father who has tied us more closely together.
Beneficence is the loveliest of duties;
He saw us perform it with ardor
And crowns us with an affectionate hand.

2. Thanks also to the throng
That formerly watched over us,

Kindled the flame of virtue
And was an example to us,
From each of whose steps on their Masonic path
There jetted a fountain of fraternal welfare.
CHORUS: The most fervent and active attempt
To raise ourselves to their level
Is the most splendid thanks to all.
Thus, let us, tripling our strength,
Undertake the lofty business,
And let the happy song fall silent.

Zum Schluss der ☐ (For the Closing of ☐; text by
Augustin Veith von Schlittersberg)

1. You, our new leaders,
Now we too thank you for your loyalty;
Continue always to lead us on the path of virtue,
So that every man rejoices in the chain
That attaches him to better people
And sweetens life's cup for him.
CHORUS: With a sacred oath we too pledge
To add to the great building like you.

2. On the pinions of truth
Raise us higher to Wisdom's throne,
So that we may reach her shrine
And become worthy of her crown,
When you yourselves benevolently through us
Dispel the envy of the uninitiated. *

*The last two lines are a makeshift translation; the German text may be corrupt here.

Das Bändchen (The Little Ribbon; text by the composer)

SOPRANO: Dear hubby,
    Where is the ribbon?
TENOR: Inside the room
    It shines and gleams.
SOPRANO: Light my way.
TENOR: Yes, yes, yes,
    I'm already here and already there.
BASS: Say, what in the world are they looking for,
    A piece of bread or a cake?
TENOR: Do you have it yet?
SOPRANO: No, go away!
TENOR: Now, now, now!
BASS: This is too impudent!
    Dear people, may I be so bold
    As to ask you what you're looking for?
SOPRANO & TENOR: Beat it!
BASS: Oh, my!
SOPRANO & TENOR: Get lost!
BASS: Oh, my!
    I'm such a good-hearted soul,
    You can twist me around your finger!
SOPRANO & TENOR: Now go!
BASS: Oh, no!
    Look, I bet I can help you out,
    For I'm a native Viennese!
SOPRANO & TENOR Our compatriot?
    Yes, nothing must be hidden from him,
    But everything must be narrated clearly.
BASS: Yes, I agree! Well, let me hear!
    Damn it, let me hear
    Or the two of you can go to the devil!

SOPRANO & TENOR: Just be patient, harsh man! We are looking
        for the beautiful ribbon.
BASS: The ribbon? Hm, now I have it in my hand.
SOPRANO & TENOR: Dear young man!
BASS: Hold your tongue!
SOPRANO & TENOR: Out of gratitude . . .
BASS: I have no time, . . .
SOPRANO & TENOR: I will always love you.
BASS: It's already late, I still have far to go.
ALL: What rapture,
      Noble sun,
      To live in true *amicitia* [friendship],
      And we have the beautiful ribbon, too,
      We have it, we have it, yes!

Grazie agl'inganni tuoi (Thanks to Your Deceits; text by Pietro Metastasio, 1698–1782, from the libretto *La libertà di Nice*)

Thanks to your deceits
At last I breathe easily, O Nice,
At last the gods had pity
On an unhappy man.
And don't be offended by the truth:
In your lovely looks
I now discover a few flaws
That used to seem beautiful to me.

Un moto di gioja (A Movement of Joy; text perhaps by Lorenzo da Ponte, 1749–1835; German translation by Daniel Jäger)

ITALIAN:
A movement of joy I feel in my breast
That announces pleasure
In the midst of fear!
Let us hope that distress will end up as contentment,
Fate and Love
Are not always tyrants.

GERMAN:
My loving heart is already pounding with joy,
Already I timorously foresee my blissful fate!
Soon my sorrow will change to rapture,
Love and Fortune are not eternally cruel.

Cantate: "Die ihr des unermesslichen Weltalls" (You Who . . . of the Measureless Universe; text by Franz Heinrich Ziegenhagen, 1753–1806)

You who honor the Creator of the measureless universe, who call him Jehovah or God, who call him Fu or Brahma, hear! hear words from the trumpet [trombone] of the universal ruler! Its eternal tone resounds loudly through planets, moons and suns; you, too, mankind, hear it!

Love Me in My works! Love order, regularity and harmony! Love yourselves and your brothers! Let physical strength and beauty be your adornment, clearness of understanding your nobility! Stretch out the fraternal hand of eternal friendship to one another, which a mere delusion—never the truth—has deprived you of for so long! Smash the bonds of this delusion, rip to shreds the veil of this prejudice, free yourselves from the garment that has disguised humanity in the form of multiple sects! Convert into plowshares the iron that hitherto has spilled the blood of men, of brothers! Blow apart rocks with the black powder that has often murderously propelled lead into the heart of a brother!

Do not imagine that true misfortune exists on My earth! It is merely a lesson, which is beneficial when it spurs you to better deeds, but which you, people, transform into misfortune when in your foolish blindness you press backward against the goad that is meant to drive you forward.

Just be wise, be strong and be brothers! Then My entire pleasure shall rest upon you, then only tears of joy will moisten your cheeks, then your laments will become sounds of jubilation, then you will turn deserts into the vales of Eden, then everything in nature will smile upon you, then it will be attained, life's true happiness.

Daphne, deine Rosenwangen (Daphne, Your Rosy Cheeks; text possibly by Friedrich Wilhelm Weiskern)

1. Daphne, your rosy cheeks
I am to see again tomorrow!
You alone are my desire,
With you I can scoff at gold.
Away with majesty, away with treasures,
They arouse no wishes in me.
Only Daphne can delight me,
I am happy only when with her.

2. Princes would envy me
If they knew all my happiness.
My triumph gives higher joys
Than the laurel wreath of heroes.
To love each other forever remains
Our sweet duty.
With such fiery, pure urges
We have no lack of happiness.

Die grossmüthige Gelassenheit (Noble Calm; text by Johann Christian Günther, 1695–1723)

I have long maintained:
Much as everything tortures me,
My spirit is not cowed by troubles;
Hope is my shield,
And when disfavor clamors,
I seek comfort in myself and remain the man I am.

Geheime Liebe (Secret Love; text by Johann Christian Günther)

What I kiss in my thoughts
Makes my life sweet
And makes sorrow and time pass.
Nor shall anyone learn of it,
I shall divulge it to no one
But mute solitude.

Die Zufriedenheit im niedrigen Stande (Contentment with a Humble Lot; text by Friedrich Rudolf Ludwig von Canitz, 1654–1699)

I do not aspire to things
That are lofty and too perilous;
My spirit never seeks to force its way
Except where it encounters easy paths.
I rest peacefully until morning,
While many a man who, full of cares,
Anxiously struggles for a vain hope,
Offers incense to the blind goddess.

Ridente la calma (May Smiling Calm; anon. Italian text and German translation by Daniel Jäger)

ITALIAN:

May smiling calm
Awaken
In my soul;
Nor let there remain
A trace
Of anger and fear.
Meanwhile, come, darling, to tighten
The sweet chains
So pleasing to my heart.

GERMAN:

The sylph of peace accompanies my life;
No cloud of worry troubles my clear gaze.
And this companion *you* gave to me,
You tender friend, I owe my happiness to you.

Wiegenlied (Lullaby; text attributed to Friedrich Wilhelm Gotter, 1746–1797)

1. Sleep, my little prince, now
   Little sheep and birds are at rest,
   Garden and meadow are silent,
   Not even a little bee is buzzing any more;
   The moon with her silvery beams
   Is looking in at the window.
   Sleep in the silvery beams,
   Sleep, my little prince, fall asleep!

2. Everyone in the palace is already in bed,
   All rocked into slumber;
   No little mouse is stirring any more,
   Cellar and kitchen are empty;
   Only in the maid's room
   Can be heard a languishing "Ah!"
   What sort of "Ah!" can it be?
   Sleep, my little prince, fall asleep!

3. Who is more fortunate than you?
   Nothing but pleasure and repose,
   Toys and candy in plenty,
   And also dashing coaches,
   Everything arranged and in readiness,
   Just so my little prince won't yell.
   What will the future be like?
   Sleep, my little prince, fall asleep!